Words Once Written:
A Collection of Poems I Tried to Write

By
Rebekah Jordan

For Ashley,

    who encourages every word

For Bill,

    who encourages every breath

The last swallow of whiskey.

He wraps his plump lips around the bottle and tips it back; his neck lengthening, his eyes closing. He fills his mouth with the last drops and pulls the empty glass away; a slight pop reaching my ears as the bottle leaves his lips.

He takes a moment to enjoy it, rolling the burning amber around his numbed tongue before swallowing slowly.

My eyes glass over as I watch his throat contract, each muscle moving in a perfect dance as my mind fills with dirty thoughts.

A single, glistening droplet clings to his lips and my breath catches. I lean forward, my hand falling to rest against his denim covered thigh, my lips parting, begging for a taste.

Green eyes turn to me and lighten with a smile.

"What're you lookin' at?" he asks, his voice thick and his tongue slow.

There's no answer that could define the beauty I'm staring at, so a kiss will have to do. I close the space between us and catch the last drop of whiskey with my lips, dabbing my tongue at the corner of his mouth.

"Delicious…"

My whisper is cut short as he turns and grabs me, his hand reaching up to cup the nape of my neck. His kiss is wet and sloppy, his hand burns against your skin.

"So are you," he teases and goes in for another.

It's gonna be a good night…

I want the warmth of his arms.

I want his breath against my neck.

I want his lips against my lips and his fingers in my hair.

I want the sweep of his tongue and the press of his hips.

I want emerald eyes gazing into my soul.

I want a voice so deep it resonates in my bones.

I want gentle touches and nipping teeth, exploring hands and his hungry mouth.

I want whispered 'I Love You's and my name on a scream.

I want his heart and his love because he has mine.

I want him.

I have lived a thousand years today
and sailed a hundred seas

    I have climbed the highest mountains
    and fallen hard onto my knees

Now I crash into my lover's arms,
warm and safe and deep

    I sink into her darkened world
    and hide myself from sleep

I think about you when my mind gets quiet,
you're always stalking the background.
I think about you and I want to feel the blade,
cut out my guilt and learn how to breathe
again.
I think about you when my chest gets tight,
when my hands are still, when my eyes are
wide.
I think about you and I drown my sorrows

I wonder if you think about me.

You're all I need to get by.
You're that first breath of air when I step outside.
You are light and shadow and hope and fear.
You're my definition of beauty and all that is real.
I love you.

If these hands were not so cold

I would not know they were my own

Unfamiliar touch

Warmth from your skin

Breath, life, love
I cannot comprehend

Tears or blood
My soles are wet from you
Deep or shallow
I still sink down

                    Guilty steps
                    Guilty heart
          Have I broken us for good?

I just wish you wanted me the
way I want you
Wish your fingertips froze for
lack of holding me
Wish that your lips would crack
without my kiss
Wish that your heart would
break if I turned away
Just wish someone wanted me
the way I want you

To be taken by passion
Ripped apart by lust
Seen through devoted eyes
Touched by burning hands
Taste me on your lips when we part and beg
for me
Think of me tomorrow and beyond,
dreaming of laying me down

Want me

     Need me

       Take me

       I'm yours.

the hard truth is,
I want so much to be alone and sit in silence
but when that happens
very bad things creep into my head.

it's never silent,

but it's only me.

Did I give in?

Perhaps.

Is all forgiven?

Never.

Hit the floor

Feel the cold seeping in

Giving up would feel

s o

g o o d

I have loved

harder than I thought possible,

a soul I will never meet.

When I'm alone
I run to you.

When the world is closing in
I cling to you.

When my mind is a mess and my blood is
screaming,
I lose myself in you.

Please don't close your arms to me.

And when I'm left alone
My mind starts to wander
To thoughts of you

I wish I could erase you
But the damage you caused
Only made me stronger

To wake up in your arms
        Wrapped in safety
To lay in comfort and the warmth of you
        Listen to the rain
To let myself go, cry, feel, release
        Trust again
                Baby, that's all I ever
                need

Some
days
I
sit
by
the
window

Listening for the engine's roar

Waiting
for
my
rescue
that
never
ever
comes

It's none too often
but I still think of you,
on these nights when the dark
seems darker.
Wonder where you are
and if you are
ever awake thinking only of me.

Can we just leave here?
Hit the gas and drive.
Tell no one where we're going
Take a breath and feel

alive…

I'm sorry for the things I said
Or so often failed to do.
I'm sorry that the love I gave
Was not enough for you.

I shouldn't be surprised
That it happened again.

> But I should be shocked
> That I didn't see it coming.

There is not enough whiskey to calm this
feeling,
This aching twitch that snakes through my
veins.
There is not enough distance to shake this
yearning,
This pulse that echoes in my brain.
I want to run to you with open arms;
Wanna fall and let you break me.
I want to scream until my throat grows
numb;
Wanna bleed and let you take me.
There is not enough whiskey to calm my
soul, to ease my mind, still my heart.
Whatever it is,
There's never enough.

29 hours alone together

I should have died
suffocating in your arms
but instead I dreamt and breathed like I
never have before.

29 hours alone together
I should have left
but I couldn't make myself leave
I couldn't, didn't want to move and inch that
would take your eyes off of me

29 hours alone together
you should have kicked me out
but now you've really done it.
I hope you're as crazy
as I know I'm becoming.

29 hours alone together

                I should have cried
        locked together, confined forever
             but I felt safe, held tight.

29 hours alone together

            I should have told the world
                so weird, so real
          I can smell you on my skin

29 hours alone together

              if you don't love me now
                 you never will
             if you don't hate me now

       you really never will

I miss you so much right now, I want to claw
my eyes out-
       they hold too many memories of you.
I need you so bad tonight, I want to peel my
skin off-
       it too clearly remembers your touch.
I need you like water, like I need my next
breath.
       But I'll hold out until it passes,
            this craving that can't be met.

I want to be kissed

                              Slowly.

I want the tingling approach,
the hesitant lift of fingers to my cheek.

        I want a gentle press of lips and the quick
        breath that comes from surprise when the
                              kiss is returned.

I want the brush of thumbs over my jaw,
a hand pushing through my hair.

    I want softly closing eyes and a racing heart.

            I want to be kissed.

I write because he haunts me.

When I need him, he's there, just over my
shoulder reaching in with a hug and a a kiss.

When my hands are still I can feel him, his
fingers close around mine, holding tight.

When my mind is quiet I can hear his voice and
he knows my name.

He's the ghost in my brain, the whispers on the
wind.

He follows me always, holding me up, pushing
me forward when I've got nothing left.

I write because he needs me to fix him, needs me
to make it alright.

I write because he's my heart and I can't leave
him alone.

I write because his story is carved into my soul.

He'll never leave me; I'll never let him go.
I write because he haunts me.

The whiskey burns;
  The steel is cold.
The blood is warm;
  My mouth is dry.

On
  and
    on
      and
        on we go

Round in this stupid game

Don't think that I've forgotten
  Don't assume that I can't bleed
Just because you're not looking
  Doesn't mean either of us are free

I would fall asleep in your loving arms

but I'm pretty sure

you don't want me anymore.

I dream in black and white;
No color but the light in your eyes.
I dream of blood and pain;
Heartbroken tears that fall like rain.
I wake in a flood of fear
Not understanding what my mind has
revealed.

I reach for you, a touch to calm my heart,

But your pillow is empty;

the room cold and dark.

Like the moon above, you brighten my way;
   Without you, I know, I'd be lost for days.

I need your smile
      Need your light
I need your arms
      To hold me tight.
I need you, baby…
      I need you tonight.

If I fall
Would you pick me up?
Is there anyone even there?

I feel the pull, feel it's grip;
Taste the empty and the nothing on my
tongue.
Can't reach up, can't call out;
I'll just let it drag me down.

And then, at night, when the world is quiet,
My mind is filled with thoughts of you.

I feel shadows
Creeping up from behind.
To cover me,
Shroud my heart and my mind.
I feel them coming,
Know their ways, see the signs.
I can't stop them,
Just pray they leave quickly this time.

I still have trouble, still fail to see
How you can do something wrong, yet the
guilty one's still me.
Maybe this is my sickness;
The guilt is written on my bones.
Paranoia is my only friend,
Its insanity, my home.

My heart hurts

      My head is a mess

My throat is tight and closing

                    Eyes unfocused

Mouth is too dry

      Another day spent asking 'why?'

Need you to hold me close tonight.
Wrap me in your arms.
Crush me next to your heart;
it's where I belong.

I never promised I was anything good, never
even tried to pretend.
Two million strangers might be wrong, but
not two of my closest friends.
So maybe I'm just poison, slowly taking you
by surprise.
Make you dizzy, make you think its love,
until you finally realize
I'm wrong
For you
I'm not
Any good
I'm a thing that takes and bleeds.
I'm an exit sign, but the door is locked;
Better just to turn and run away.

My Alone is screaming
Violent words of hate that swirl through my
head.

My Alone is empty
Knowing I'm nothing; maybe better of dead.

My Alone is pain
That grips my heart and pierces my lungs.

My Alone is a crowd
Faces that all want me; none of them the
truth.

My Alone is forever
And sadly, nothing new.

Show me your smile, let me see you shine.
I need your arms wrapped tight around
mine.

                    I want your heart beating hard,
                        your hands moving slow.

    We can take our time, I got nowhere to go

I'm sorry if you thought I was more
Sorry if you hurt because of me
I'm sorry that I wasn't good enough
Sorry if you cried over me
I'm sorry if I wasn't what you needed
Wasn't what you wanted in the end
I'm sorry that I'm not better
I'm sorry that I'm just me

I hate the way the world turns;

you come and you go so easily it burns.

My heart was open only for you

and you took what you wanted like you

always do.

I should have seen it coming,

should just let it go;

but I miss you.

and

I really hope

you'll never know.

Words, once spoken,

       dissolve into the breeze.

But written here they cut,
                  sting,
                        burn,
                              freeze.

I wrote you a letter once,
explaining the whys against and the maybes
for.

I folded it carefully and shoved it in a
drawer,
wrote your name in blue ink on the front.

I wrote it all down so I didn't have to tell
you,
afraid to say the words aloud, see you turn
and walk away.

I left it there, in the back of that drawer
amongst the batteries and rubber bands.

I wrote you a letter once that I never needed.

We rewrote the questions and found our
answers

Together.

I like how it takes so long
        for my breath to reach the flame
and how today you acted like
        you'd never seen my face

Sometimes I ask myself
        if sleep is worth the dreams
Sometimes I stay awake for days wondering

If you're worth it.

The ballfield was empty when I passed it today and I thought of you.

I want to be snuggled in between a wall of
pillows and a wall of you.

Trapped on all sides by softness and warmth.

I want your hand in the curve of my waist
and your nose against mine.

I want our breaths to mix and our eyes to
close.

I want our knees to fight for the comfiest spot
and our fingers to lock.

I want a blanket over our heads when the
light gets too bright

and a whispering promise that everything
will be alright.

It was the car. Seats that baked in the sun, cracking under his thighs and burning his hands. The steering wheel that was soft and worn by years of touch, the black lightened to gray where his thumb rubbed daily.

It was his jacket. Loved and worn only occasionally now; the last piece of his younger days. It fit a little tighter now around the middle and the cuffs fell perfectly at his wrists where once they hung low.

It was his father's journal. Kept hidden away now, but often returned to, scanned over by misty eyes and sad fingertips simply longing for the closeness that his father's handwriting offered. There were pictures tucked into the cover and random scribbles that he knew by heart.

It was the belt that often held a gun against his back and the blackness of his shoes.

It was a rectangle that held his badge and the sheath for his knife.

It was the chairs in the library where he sat to think and to learn. The books he poured over, ancient in their bindings and more so in their wisdom.

It was part of almost everything he touched and as the years ticked by, he found leather in the mirror.

It was in the roughness of his cheek and the cracks near his eyes.

It was his hands, worn like the steering wheel, rough yet soft.

It was his voice, deeper than ever, yet still warm and familiar.

Leather surrounded him, warmed him, became him. He was tough and cracked and worn, but soft and strong.

He was leather.

2018
Cover Design by Rebekah Jordan
Photography by Jennifer Bishop

19743645R00057

Made in the USA
Middletown, DE
07 December 2018